THE HUTCHINSON
BOOK OF
CAT
TALES

HUTCHINSON

London Sydney Auckland Johannesburg

THE HUTCHINSON BOOK OF CAT TALES
A HUTCHINSON BOOK 0 09 189321 6

Published in Great Britain by Hutchinson,
an imprint of Random House Children's Books

This edition published 2004

1 3 5 7 9 10 8 6 4 2

RANDOM HOUSE CHILDREN'S BOOKS
61–63 Uxbridge Road, London W5 5SA
A division of The Random House Group Ltd

RANDOM HOUSE AUSTRALIA (PTY) LTD
20 Alfred Street, Milsons Point, Sydney,
New South Wales 2061, Australia

RANDOM HOUSE NEW ZEALAND LTD
18 Poland Road, Glenfield, Auckland 10, New Zealand

RANDOM HOUSE (PTY) LTD
Endulini, 5A Jubilee Road, Parktown 2193, South Africa

THE RANDOM HOUSE GROUP Limited Reg. No. 954009
www.kidsatrandomhouse.co.uk

A CIP catalogue record for this book is available from the British Library.

Printed in Hong Kong

Contents

The Patchwork Cat

William Mayne and Nicola Bayley

"Good morning, good yawning," says Tabby, getting up.
She stretches.

She sleeps on a quilt. It is patchwork, like herself.
She loves it.

She loves her breakfast too.
She waits for it.

She says good morning
and good yawning to
the people who live
in her house.

They are a mother and a father and two children.

They all watch for the milkman. Tabby's tail begins to twitch.

They hear his float, they hear him sing.

Tabby goes out and loves the milkman.

"Oh milkman, milkman," she says, "you can come and live at my house any time."

Milk is poured for her.

After breakfast Tabby goes to have another little rest.

But she cannot find the patchwork quilt, her matching, patchwork quilt.

"Ah," says the mother, "we have done some snatchwork on your patchwork. We have thrown it out because it is so very dirty, and we shall buy a basket."

Tabby does not want a basket. She will do some angry scratchwork on it if it comes.

"I think I should send this family away," she says. "I shall have the milkman here to lodge instead."

She goes to look for her patchwork quilt, to wash herself and stretch and sleep.

She finds it. It is in the rubbish bin. She reaches up and touches it. She climbs in under the lid with it, and goes to sleep.

Then bang and crash, and black and thick the dark.

The lid is tightly on,
the bin is in the air and
upside-down. Tabby falls out,
wrapped in her patchwork quilt.

She is in the rubbish truck.
She sits and cries with no one there
to hear. The engines and the shaking
and the dangers and the quaking
catch her calls.

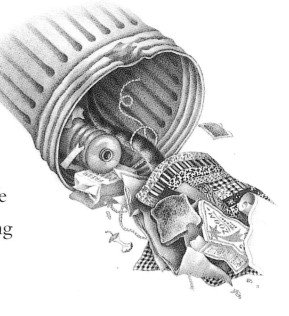

She is going on a journey.
She is scared. She does not
like it much.

She hisses and she arches up
her back, but no one knows.

The journey ends. The truck
lifts up its back and hisses.
It tips out Tabby and her
patchwork quilt.

Where she is she cannot
tell. There is nothing good
to see and nothing good
to smell.

She does not like to touch.
She sees that all this place
is rubbish. She has to dodge
aside, here comes another batch.

And then another, until the day is over.

The last truck goes; the driver
latches up the gate.

Tabby is in the dump and
cannot get out.

She says, "I am a sorry wretch."

Darkness comes. Rats wake up and gnash their teeth at her and flash their eyes.

They watch and make her rage with fright. She guards her patchwork quilt all night, and growls and squalls.

At morning time the rats go home. The gates are opened once again. The trucks begin to pitch the rubbish in.

Tabby drags her patchwork quilt up to the gate. She will not let it go.

She waits until a truck has left, and with her quilt she follows up the track.

She hopes a truck will not
come by and crush the
patchwork quilt or crunch
her bones. She crawls
along the ditch.

She holds a corner
of the patchwork in her
mouth, and has to clench her teeth.

She comes safely out. But she is far from home and does not
know how long she'll have to trudge.

She will not go without the
patchwork quilt.

Her teeth begin to ache.
She goes along a street
and does not know the
way. Each turning might
be wrong. Which one to
take she cannot tell.
She hopes she does not
meet a cruel dog or bitch.

Then she hears a sound
she knows, and the voice
she loves the best.
Her tail begins
to twitch.

The milkman in his float is
there, the rich voice sings
a morning song.

"Good morning," says
the milkman, "here's Tabby
far from home and lost.
Come up with me, and
I'll soon fetch you to
your kitchen, with your
pretty patchwork quilt that's
all the fashion."

Tabby sits beside him on her patchwork quilt, and licks herself.

The milkman pours fresh milk to drink. Tabby is hitch-hiking home.

At home the mother and the father and the children are very pleased to see that she is found.

Tabby thinks that they can stay, if the milkman will promise to come each day.

The mother says that she must wash the patchwork quilt to make it fresh, and mend it with a stitch or two to make it new.

Tabby says, "I'll be tired soon, so wash it now."

When it's clean she sleeps till dinner time, then wakes and says, "Good morning, good yawning," and has a great big stretch.

She makes sure she is home, and goes to sleep again all afternoon.

Big Tom and Fluff

Shirley Isherwood and Rimantas Rolia

Fluff came into Big Tom's garden.
He was wearing his blue jacket. But
his owner had put it on back to front.

"If I want to sneeze, I won't be able to get my handkerchief," he said to Big Tom.

"Don't worry, Fluff," said Big Tom. "If you feel that you are going to sneeze, I will get your handkerchief for you."

Big Tom is a good friend, thought Fluff.

SMASH! BANG! WALLOP!
SNUFFLE! GRUNT!

"What's that?" asked Fluff, hiding behind Big Tom.

"It's our new neighbour," said Big Tom gravely. "He sounds very fierce."

"Oh, dear," said Fluff. "I hope he stays over his side of the garden."

"Don't worry," said Big Tom. "If we stay together we'll be all right."

Big Tom and Fluff sat
down in their favourite
place under the tree.

"Oh, Tom!" said Fluff.
"I think I'm going to sneeze."

Big Tom felt in the pocket
and found Fluff's handkerchief.
It was new and clean and folded
neatly and had the letter "F" stitched
in blue thread in one corner.

But before he could give it to
Fluff, a strong breeze snatched it from his paw!

"Oh no!" cried Fluff as it flew into bushes and over the fence
where the fierce new neighbour lived.

From the other side came a loud trampling
of twigs and the sound of grunting.

"Don't worry, Fluff," said Big Tom.
"I'll get your handkerchief for you!"

He padded off down the garden. By
the bushes he stopped, turned and waved.
"Try not to sneeze until I get back,"
he said. And he disappeared from view.

Fluff's eyes shone with wonder.
How brave he is, he told himself.
I am just a timid little kitten.
I could *never* go into that place.
He sat and waited quietly
beneath the tree.

"Tom?" he called after a while. Big Tom did not answer.
Fluff got up and trotted down the garden path.

As he went there came a loud snort.

And then a great crashing sound.

Smash! Bang! Wallop!

Fluff stood still.

Grunt! Grunt! Grunt! Snuffle-snort!

These are angry sounds, thought Fluff.

Something is angry at Big Tom!

Fluff peered into the dark bushes.

"You can't go there," said a little voice in his ear. "You are just a small, timid, fluffy thing."

"Go away!" said Fluff to the voice. "Tom is my friend! I must help him!"

Something grunted very loudly.

"Oh dear!" came Big Tom's voice.

Fluff tore into the bushes. As he ran he heard three loud grunts. Then three loud squeals.

And standing there was . . .

. . . a large, pink pig.

Big Tom was holding Fluff's handkerchief.

"Fluff, I'm frightened," he said. "I think he's going to *eat* me."

The pink pig snorted and stamped his foot.

"*I* think he is going to sneeze!" said Fluff.

He took the handkerchief and gave it to the pig.

"Atishoo!" went the pig. "Dank you bery mud. Bost kide!"

Then he turned and made his way back to his own garden.

Big Tom and Fluff went back to their place under the tree.

"Oh, Fluff," said Big Tom. "You were so brave!"

"So were you! Oh, Big Tom," said Fluff, "he took my handkerchief. And I think I'm going to sneeze."

"Take mine," said Big Tom and he gave Fluff his own.

It was new and clean and folded neatly and had the letter "T" stitched in blue thread in one corner.

"Atishoo!" went Fluff.

"Bless you, dear Fluff," said Big Tom.

Cloudy

Deborah King

I am a little grey cat called Cloudy.
I am the colour of thunder and rain.
It's difficult to see me on dull days.

When the rain pours, you may catch sight of me in murky puddles.
When the wind blows, I am swept away like a ball of fluff.

If the sun shines, I'll be stalking in the shadows.

When I was wild, I slept in a stable.

I lurked in tumbledown
sheds and dark alleys.

If I rolled in the dirt, I would disappear in a cloud of dust.

Now, I sit by a warm stove on a winter's evening,
but still no one knows I am there.

In the early mornings I hide
in the top of the plum tree
where the birds can't see me.

I hunt at dusk.

I prowl through the long grass under the light of the moon.

If I cross the road, I must run like the wind . . .

When I come home, I creep through my front door, silently, secretly. No one notices.

No one, that is, except my old friend, who keeps my secret until the first misty light of dawn . . .

when I disappear again.

Lazy Daisy

Rob Lewis

Daisy was a sea cat.

   She lived on a trading ship that carried grain and spices from faraway places across the oceans.

   All day she dozed amongst the ropes in the hot sun.

"That cat is lazy!" growled the captain. "All she does is eat and sleep."

Daisy opened one eye, yawned, stretched and went back to sleep.

"There are rat holes in the sails," grumbled the sailmaker.

"There are dirty rat footprints on the charts," moaned the first mate.

"There are rat teeth marks in the salt beef," complained the purser.

"Where's that useless cat?" roared the captain. "I'll throw it overboard!"

"Don't do that, captain," pleaded the cook's boy, who liked cats.

"Very well," mumbled the captain, "but unless that cat starts catching rats soon, I will sell her at the next port!"

Daisy had been sitting on the
yardarm, listening.

She didn't want to be a land cat.

She loved the sea life.

She would have to catch some rats.

Down in the hold, she prowled
amongst the sacks trying to look
fierce. Perhaps the rats would be
frightened away. The rats sat on
top of a pile of barrels, laughing.

"Stupid, lazy cat," they said.

One rat nibbled a hole in a sack.

Out poured a stream of flour onto Daisy's head.

"Useless cat!" scowled the purser, when he saw Daisy.

The cook's boy gave Daisy some cheese.

"See if you can catch some
rats with this," he said.

Daisy climbed into
a coil of rope and
waited for a rat to
come and nibble
at the cheese.

"Stupid, lazy cat," laughed the rats.
They scurried up the mast and gnawed
through the ropes that held one of the sails.
Down it came on top of Daisy.

"Asleep again?" sighed the sailmaker, when he found Daisy.

Daisy crept down to the very bottom of the ship and sniffed for rat holes amongst the brandy casks.

"Stupid, lazy cat," said the rats. They pulled the bungs out of some casks.

"Drunken cat!" hissed the first mate, when he found Daisy in a pool of brandy.

"The rats on this ship are worse than ever!" said the captain.
"Tomorrow in port I shall sell that cat!"

Poor Daisy. She had never caught a rat before and these were
very clever rats.

That night there was a terrible storm. Wind battered the sails
and waves crashed over the decks.

The first mate was at the wheel. Suddenly he was washed across the deck.

The captain came to help the first mate.

"We must steer the ship away from the rocks," said the captain. Together they struggled to get to the wheel against the wind and waves.

"We shall all be drowned!" wailed the first mate.

Then, through the rain, they saw the wheel.

"Look at that!" said the captain.

"I don't believe it!" said the first mate.

There was Daisy holding the wheel steady
with her paws.

She had saved the ship from hitting the rocks.

"Clever cat," said the
sailmaker, the next morning.
"Brave cat!" said the purser.

"Well done, Daisy," said the cook's boy.

"I certainly won't sell you," said the captain,
and he placed his cap on Daisy's head.

She felt very proud.

And what happened to the rats?

During the storm – like all cowardly rats . . .

. . . they left the sinking ship!

The Megamogs

Peter Haswell

In a quaint little old house lived a quaint little old lady called Miss Marbletop. Miss Marbletop collected mogs. And she had a whole mighty, magnificent, mindless, moronic, mog-eared mob of them. They were called Miss Marbletop's Megamogs.

It was on Monday morning that Miss Marbletop went off in her old, red sports car.

It was on Monday afternoon that Kevin Catflap, Captain of the Megamogs, addressed the others.

"Right," said Kevin Catflap. "We're going to paint the house."

"I vote we paint it pink," said Tracy Tinopener.

"Green," growled Fishpaste Fred.

"Puce," piped up Phil Fleacollar.

"Red!" shouted Ginger Brownsauce and Gary Gristle.

"ORDER! ORDER!" cried Kevin Catflap. "Never mind the colour – JUST PAINT!"

And so the Megamogs painted Miss Marbletop's House.

And this is how it looked.

"Great!" exclaimed Kevin Catflap. "Nice paintwork. Now, I want everyone in bed early. Tomorrow we've got real work to do – so no going out on the tiles. No serenading or parading. No dustbin bashing, bottle smashing, rooting tooting alley-scooting, caterwauling, bawling or squalling. I want everybody up and awake, bright eyed and bushy tailed, ready to give it some welly tomorrow at seven. Right?"

"What's the job, Kev?" asked Barry Binliner.

"I'm not saying yet," said Kevin, darkly. "But it's going to be BIG!"

7.00 a.m. Tuesday. The Megamogs put on their hard hats . . .

Then they brought in diggers, dumpers, bulldozers, picks, shovels, cement mixers, cones, signs and . . .

They built a mighty highway right past the front of Miss Marbletop's house.

"Great!" pronounced Kevin Catflap. "Nice highway. Now – early to bed and early to rise. No all nighting, fighting or moonlighting. No howling, yowling or prowling. I want you all here, up with the larks, whisker sharp and raring to go tomorrow at seven."

"What's the plan, Kev?" asked Glitzy Mitzy.

"I'll give you a clue," said Kevin. "It's going to be BIG!"

7.00 a.m. Wednesday. The Megamogs put on their overalls . . .

Then they dug foundations, drove piles, brought in cranes, raised girders high into the sky, heaved, hauled, sweated, strained and built . . .

An enormous office block right behind Miss Marbletop's house.

"Great!" declared Kevin Catflap. "Nice office block. Now – everyone gets an early night. Right? No partying, prancing and dancing. No disco diving, go-go jiving, boogie bopping, night-spot hopping. We've got to be up and at 'em, on the ball and tails tingling at sparrow squeak tomorrow."

"OK, Kev," said Derek Dogbender. "What's the deal this time?"

"You'll see," said Kevin Catflap. "It's going to be BIG! "

7.00 a.m. Thursday. The Megamogs put on their workboots.

Then they humped, heaved, dragged, dug, drilled, moiled, toiled, boiled, huffed, puffed, grumbled, groused, growled, groaned, bellyached and built . . .

A huge airport behind the office block at the back of Miss Marbletop's house.

"Great!" grinned Kevin Catflap. "Nice airport. Now tonight we're going to—"

"Forget it, Kev!" cut in Sardine Sid. "Tonight we're going out – tom catting, high hatting, go-go dancing, disco prancing, rapping, rocking, hip hopping, scene stopping and big bopping. We're going to party till we're pooped!"

"That's what I was about to say," said Kevin. "Tonight we'll have a night out on the tiles. So come on, everybody. Let's get on down and boogie!"

This is the night out on the tiles that the Megamogs had.

"Great!" gasped Kevin Catflap. "Nice night out. Now, I've got an announcement to make – today, Miss Marbletop comes home. So no dozing, dreaming or dodging. We're going to lay on a reception and it's going to be BIG!"

This is the reception Miss Marbletop came home to.

Then, when she looked at her house . . .

This is what Miss
Marbletop saw.

And this is what she said:

"Oh my gosh! Oh my goodness! Oh my sainted aunt! Great Scott! Good heavens! By George! By jove! By jingo! Saints preserve us! Oh flip! Well I never did! Stone the crows! Blow me down! Who would believe it! Great balls of fire . . .

"I LOVE IT!"

And the Megamogs?

They flew off from the airport for the holiday of a lifetime.

ONE WEEK LATER

"Great!" said Kevin Catflap. "Nice holiday. But tonight I want you all in bed early. No misbehaving, raving or midnight bathing, because tomorrow, we're going to do something.

"And guess what.

"It's going to be . . .

The Cat That Scratched

Jonathan Long and Korky Paul

There once was a cat with a terrible itch.

She had a flea in her fur which was making her twitch.

She scratched herself here
and she scritched herself there.
She scritched
upside down
and she scratched
in mid air.

She whirled her paws fast
and she span like a top,
Then fell head over heels
and she rolled to a stop.

"Ha ha ha," said a voice, all tiny and teasy.
"To get rid of me won't be nearly that easy."

"You talkative tickle," said the cat. "You bothersome bug!"
"When I've finished with you,
you won't sound
so smug."

SCRITCH
SCRATCH SCRITCH
SCRATCH SCRATCH
SCRITCH SCRATCH
SCRATCH SCRATCH
SCRATCH

So she went to the cupboard in one of the rooms
And found a big hoover amongst all the brooms.

She plugged in the plug and she flicked on the switch,
And said, "Say your prayers, you tortuous titch."

She hoovered her tum and her ears and her nose,
And each one of her legs right down to her toes.

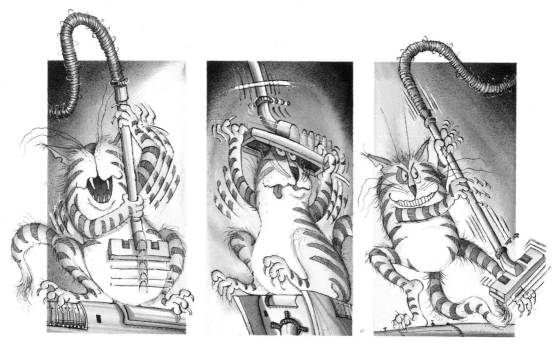

But catastrophe struck – her tail was sucked in,
And the hoover exploded with
a deafening din!

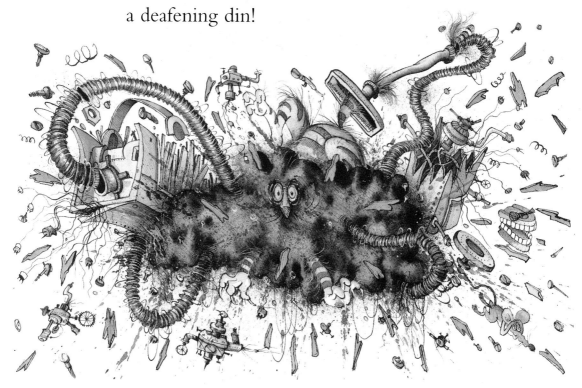

When she opened her eyes, she was flat on the ceiling,
An unusual position which was most unappealing.

"Ha ha ha," said a voice, all tiny and teasy.
"To get rid of me won't be nearly that easy."

"You nigglesome nit!" said the cat. "You mischievous mite!
I'm really mad now so get set for a fight."

So she ran down the road to a friendly hairdresser
Who wore a pink gown and was called Trendy Tessa.

"Listen, Tess,"
said the cat.
"Keep this
hush-hush,
There's an itch
in my fur
and I need
a good brush."

So Tess combed her all over with a big spiky comb,
And curled her and clipped her and sprayed her with foam.

But when it was done, the poor cat looked a fright,
And can you believe it – she felt a small bite!

"Ha ha ha," came a voice, all tiny and teasy.
"To get rid of me won't be nearly that easy."

"You loudmouthed louse!" said the cat. "You pernickety pest!
I'm going to put you to the ultimate test."

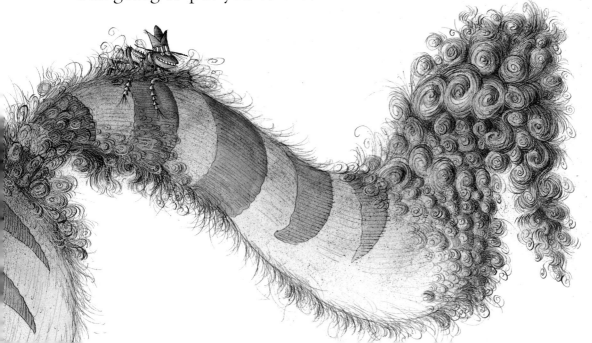

So she went to a carwash and paid 50p,
To a fat man in jeans who was drinking some tea.

Then she dived right inside a very large washer,
Which had rollers and soapers and a powerful splosher.

Scruba-dub-dub, it went, duba-scrub-scrub,
And rolled her around like a sock in a tub.

But she swallowed some water which made her all soggy,
And she had to leap out; a water-logged moggy.

"Ha ha ha," came a voice, all tiny and teasy.
"To get rid of me won't be nearly that easy."

"Oh dear," wailed the cat, feeling awfully poorly,
"It looks like I'm stuck with this
darned creepy-crawly."

SCRATCH SCRITCH SCRITCH
SCRITCH SCRITCH SCRATCH
SCRITCH SCRATCH
SCRITCH SCRATCH
SCRATCH SCRATCH
SCRATCH SCRATCH
SCRATCH
SCRITCH

But just then she heard shouts and a hullaballoo:
Her cousin the lion had escaped from the zoo.

"Hey, puss," yelled the lion, with a big friendly smile,
"Have you got a place I might hide for a while?"

But before she could answer they heard a small pop,
The flea had moved house with a seven-yard hop.

"Goodbye, cat," it shouted and waved a small hanky,
"You're a fright, you're a mess, you're matted and manky.

"You're frizzled and frazzled and far too run down.
So I'm trading you in for the top cat in town."

But with an elegant hitch the lion lifted its paw,
Flicked out the flea and squashed it flat on the floor.

"Grrr," said the lion, "that flea didn't half bungle.
Nobody messes with the King of the Jungle."

"Silly me," said the cat, "no one needs tricks.
Just trust your family if you're in a fix."

So she invited him home, and they put up a sign,
Which spelled out in big letters:
BEWARE OF THE LION.

Then they fell fast asleep with their tails all curled,
The two happiest cats you could meet in the world.

Bottomley the Brave

Peter Harris and Doffy Weir

It doesn't take much to wake me.

So I was on my feet the moment the six burglars broke in.
Of course, they knew they'd made a big mistake as soon
as they saw me.

"Quick! Run for it!" one burglar screamed.

"That's no ordinary cat! That's Bottomley!

"Bottomley the Brave."

But I wasn't going to let them get away that easily.

They asked for this, Bottomley, I told myself.

And now they're going to get it.

I was on them in a second, clawing and biting.

Well, the fight didn't last long.

Because I don't think they'd met a cat who knew karate before.
And pretty soon four of them were begging for mercy.

The other two tried to run for it. But they didn't stand a chance.
Who would against a trained fighting cat like me?

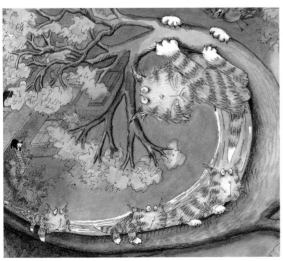

And then I just rang for the police to come and arrest them.

But the bad news is, while I was clobbering the last two
burglars, the other four ate that roast chicken you were
saving for supper and escaped.

"You believe me, don't you?"

"No, Bottomley. Not one word.

"But we do believe you are the laziest, sleepiest, greediest, funniest cat . . .

. . . who tells the best stories in the world."

Slobcat

Paul Geraghty

Slobcat is our cat.
He does nothing but
lie about and sleep.

Heaven knows what he does
when we're not there.

But when we get home he's still sleeping.
That's why we call
him Slobcat.

When it's his dinner time, he's nowhere to be seen.
And when we *do* find him, he's even too lazy to eat.

I don't know where he goes when
we put him out. But he often comes
back soaking wet because he's too
lazy to shelter from the rain.

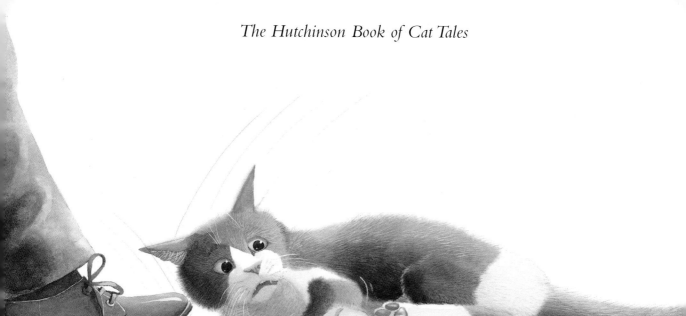

He spends so much time inside
that he ends up getting in the way!

Last week Mum saw a mouse,
so Dad put out a trap . . .

because Slobcat isn't interested in chasing mice.

All *he*'s interested in is
lying about in the sun.

Luckily, we don't
have rats . . .

because if we did,
Dad says we'd
have to get a
proper cat.

Some people have dangerous animals in their gardens. But for some reason, they don't seem to come into ours.

It's strange because the *little* creatures
don't seem afraid.

Sometimes, when we're asleep, there are burglars
about. Thank goodness we have Brutus to frighten
them off because Slobcat couldn't frighten a flea!

People say that all cats have a secret
life that we don't know about.

But I'm sure Slobcat's
much too lazy for that!

The Black and White Cat

Deborah King

The black and white cat was born in the city.

There were no trees or gardens near her home –
only an avenue of streetlights and paving stones
strewn with dirt blown up by the passing traffic.

Midnight was the safest time for the black and white cat. She prowled the dark streets until morning and then she was gone.

She never saw the sun rise.

In the late afternoon she would wake from her long sleep and look out over her dull, bleak world. She wondered what lay beyond the blue-grey hills.

One night she went further than she ever had before. She walked past the factories and the houses and on and on up the long, winding road.

When she reached the top of the hill the sun rose in a blaze of light.

But it was too bright for the black and white cat who had lived all of her life in the shadows.

Surely I don't belong in such a beautiful world, she thought.

She ran back into the shade. There she caught a glimpse of some strange wild creatures as they scuttled across the forest floor and disappeared.

And from high in the branches, two magpies flew up and up, their wings brilliant against the blue sky.

Cautiously the black and white cat crept out into the countryside. She hid in the long grass.

Even the insects are more colourful than me, she thought sadly.

Then, in the distance, she saw a herd of big, gentle creatures grazing in the sun. She crept towards them and lost herself in the patchwork pattern that stretched far across the green fields.

She followed them all the way to the farm.

But this was the home of another cat. Wild and fierce, he spat at the black and white cat.

The barn was his territory and no other creature was allowed near.

On and on went the black and white cat, until she found a place where the colours were brighter and more beautiful than ever before.

But could this be a place for an ordinary black and white cat?

She stepped out of the shadows and sat down in the garden. Her coat shone and her eyes sparkled for the first time. They were brighter than any flower.

Someone walked up softly behind the black and white cat and picked her up.

"What a lovely cat," she whispered, taking her inside.

Now every morning the black and white cat looks out over her gentle, green world . . .

. . . and in the afternoon she prowls
the countryside in all her simple beauty.

The Gondolier's Cat

William Corlett and Alicia Garcia de Lynam

Once, long ago in Venice, there lived a cat called Nini. Nini was black and sleek and had the tip of one ear missing, lost years before in a fight with an alley cat on the banks of a gloomy backwater.

Nini lived in a little house on the Grand Canal, which is the high street of Venice, with Gino the gondolier and his wife Maria.

Gino was one of the poorest men in the city and his house was falling down. He wore a special hat so that people knew he was a gondolier.

From the window of Gino's house, Nini could see the Doge's palace.

The Doge was the richest and most powerful man in all Venice. He also wore a special hat so that everyone knew who he was, but his palace was not falling down. It was the finest and largest house in the entire city.

The Doge had a daughter, whom he loved very much.
She was a beautiful princess, and kings and princes came
from all over the world to seek her hand in marriage.
But the Doge vowed that his daughter would not marry
until she herself found a man whom she could love.

The Doge's daughter had a white cat whom she
called La Serenissima. Her fur was like silk and
her eyes the colour of the sky. La Serenissima
also vowed that she would not marry until she
found a cat whom she could love.

Each day Gino and Nini waited at the quayside outside the Doge's palace for customers. Each day Nini sat in the prow of the gondola and stared up at the lovely Serenissima.

"That cat belongs to a princess," Gino told him. "She wouldn't look twice at a one-eared moggy like you, so forget her, Nini, and go and do something useful. Catch a mouse, or better still a fish, then I can share it with you."

Nini's love for
La Serenissima
made him wild
and daring.

He was so desperate
to win her that he
tried everything to
attract her attention.

But after each
and every one
of his tricks,
La Serenissima
merely yawned.

One misty morning a pirate ship stole into the lagoon on the early tide, while the city was still sleeping.

The ugly crew rowed silently across to the quay. They quickly overcame the unsuspecting guards and broke into the Doge's palace. They collected all the jewels and the silver and the valuable paintings, and even the teaspoons from the Doge's kitchen, and threw everything over the balcony to their mates down below.

Worst of all they took the beautiful princess, wrapped up in a carpet. But they were not quick enough to catch La Serenissima, who jumped between their legs and over the balcony into the piazza.

"Help! Help!" wailed La Serenissima. "Thieves! Brigands!"

Her cries reached right across the
Grand Canal to where Nini lay
sleeping, stretched out on his roof.

Nini thought he was dreaming.
Wasn't that the beautiful
Serenissima's voice?

He was so excited that he
jumped straight down off the
roof, without bothering to use the stairs.

Then he crossed the Grand Canal with a hop and a skip and three
jumps, without so much as getting his paws wet.

"Do something!" pleaded La Serenissima. "They've taken the
princess."

Nini ran to the cathedral bell tower and
climbed up it so fast that he looked more
like a squirrel than a cat. Then, pulling
with all his strength, he rang the great bell,
waking all the citizens of Venice and the
militia and even the Doge, who had had
a good dinner and was snoring soundly.

The soldiers didn't even have time
to put on their uniforms. Wearing
nothing but their nightshirts,
they chased the pirates right
round the square.

The pirates were so surprised that they dropped all their treasures, including the princess wrapped up in the carpet, and they ran for the quay.

But when they got there, they discovered that Gino and Nini had towed all their boats away and they couldn't escape back to their ship in the lagoon. So the pirates were rounded up by the soldiers and taken away to a dungeon.

The Doge gave a masked ball to celebrate the victory over the pirates. The princess danced every dance with a handsome stranger and was happier than she had ever been.

The Doge declared Nini the hero of Venice.
He ordered a special statue to be erected
in his honour.

He made Gino his personal
gondolier and gave him a
new hat to show how
important he had become.

The princess soon realized that she was in love with the handsome stranger, who was himself a prince and was already so in love with her that he had come specially to seek her hand in marriage.

La Serenissima decided that Nini was by far the bravest cat in the whole of Venice.

The princess married her prince in the cathedral of San Marco, next to the Doge's palace.

And as for Nini and La Serenissima,

they also married.

And she never yawned at his tricks again.

Acknowledgements

The publishers gratefully acknowledge the following authors and illustrators:

The Patchwork Cat published by Jonathan Cape Children's Books
Text © William Mayne, 1981   Illustrations © Nicola Bayley, 1981

Big Tom and Fluff
Text © Shirley Isherwood, 2004   Illustrations © Rimantas Rolia, 2004

Cloudy published by Hutchinson Children's Books
Text and illustrations © Deborah King, 1989

Lazy Daisy published by The Bodley Head Children's Books
Text and illustrations © Rob Lewis, 1994

The Megamogs published by The Bodley Head Children's Books
Text and illustrations © Peter Haswell, 1994

The Cat That Scratched published by The Bodley Head Children's Books
Text © Jonathan Long, 1994   Illustrations © Korky Paul, 1994
www.korkypaul.com

Bottomley the Brave published by Hutchinson Children's Books
Text © Peter Harris, 1996   Illustrations © Doffy Weir, 1996

Slobcat published by Hutchinson Children's Books
Text and illustrations © Paul Geraghty, 1991
www.paulgeraghty.net

The Black and White Cat published by Hutchinson Children's Books
Text and illustrations © Deborah King, 1993

The Gondolier's Cat published by Hodder and Stoughton Children's Books
Text © William Corlett, 1993   Illustrations in this edition © Alicia Garcia de Lynam, 2004

With special thanks to Caroline Sheldon for her help with this anthology